Teeny, Tiny MOUSE

A BOOK ABOUT COLORS

by Laura Leuck

illustrated by Pat Schories

SCHOLASTIC INC.

New York Toronto London Auckland Sydney
Mexico City New Delhi Hong Kong Buenos Aires

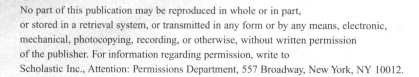

ISBN 0-439-64434-8

Text copyright © 1998 by Laura Leuck. Illustrations copyright © 1998 by Pat Schories.
All rights reserved. Published by Scholastic Inc. SCHOLASTIC, TROLL, and associated
logos and designs are trademarks and/or registered trademarks of Scholastic Inc.

12 11 10 9 8 7 6 5 4 3   10 11 12/0

Printed in the U.S.A.   40

First Scholastic printing, November 2004

Designed by Dorit Radandt
Hand lettering by Dee Dee Burnside

Teeny, Tiny
MOUSE

A BOOK ABOUT COLORS

For my wonderful parents, John and Gwen—L.L.

For the very colorful Thomas family!—P.S.

"Can you name some colors in our teeny, tiny house?"
said the teeny, tiny mommy to the teeny, tiny mouse.

"There are colored things in every room,
and I can name them, too.
Throughout our teeny, tiny house
I'll point them out to you."

"Can you name some blue things in our teeny, tiny house?"
said the teeny, tiny mommy to the teeny, tiny mouse.

"There's a blue chair in the parlor.
A blue picture on the wall.
And a teeny, tiny blue ball
rolling slowly down the hall."

"Can you name some brown things in our teeny, tiny house?"
said the teeny, tiny mommy to the teeny, tiny mouse.

"There's a brown clock on the mantel
and a brown rug on the floor.
And a teeny, tiny brown knob
on the teeny, tiny door."

"Can you name some black things in our teeny, tiny house?"
said the teeny, tiny mommy to the teeny, tiny mouse.

"There's a black pot on the table.
A black handle on a pan.
And some teeny, tiny black beans
in a teeny, tiny can."

"Can you name some orange things in our teeny, tiny house?"
said the teeny, tiny mommy to the teeny, tiny mouse.

"There's a pitcher full of orange juice.
Orange cheese for lunch.
And some teeny, tiny flowers
in a teeny, tiny bunch."

"Can you name some red things in our teeny, tiny house?"
said the teeny, tiny mommy to the teeny, tiny mouse.

"There's a red bike in the corner.
A red cushion on its seat.
And teeny, tiny red shoes
for my teeny, tiny feet."

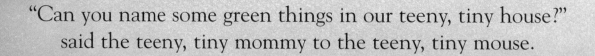

"Can you name some green things in our teeny, tiny house?"
said the teeny, tiny mommy to the teeny, tiny mouse.

"There's a green plant in the sunroom.
A green sweater that I wear.
And green teeny, tiny pillows
on the teeny, tiny chair."

"Can you name some pink things in our teeny, tiny house?"
said the teeny, tiny mommy to the teeny, tiny mouse.

"There's a pink hat on the bedpost
and pink lipstick on the stand.
And a teeny, tiny pink belt
with a teeny, tiny band."

"Can you name some white things in our teeny, tiny house?"
said the teeny, tiny mommy to the teeny, tiny mouse.

"There's a white frame 'round the mirror
and white handles on the tub.
And some teeny, tiny white soap
that I use to wash and scrub."

"Can you name some purple things
in our teeny, tiny house?"
said the teeny, tiny mommy
to the teeny, tiny mouse.

"There's a purple spread across my bed.
Purple stripes upon my walls.
And a teeny, tiny purple phone
for teeny, tiny calls."

"Can you name some yellow things
in our teeny, tiny house?"
said the teeny, tiny mommy
to the teeny, tiny mouse.

"There's a yellow roof above us
and a yellow floor below.
And a teeny, tiny candle
with a teeny, tiny glow."

"You have named the colors in our teeny, tiny house,"
said the teeny, tiny mommy to the teeny, tiny mouse.

"I know the colors one and all
as sure as I'm a mouse."

Do you know all the colors in
YOUR teeny, tiny house?